# Words with Wings

## A Treasury of African-American Poetry and Art

### selected by Belinda Rochelle

HarperCollins*Publishers*

 Amistad

**This book is dedicated to my daughter,**

**Shevon, for her love and inspiration**

Permission to reproduce poetry in this book is gratefully acknowledged: "Auction Street," "This Morning," and "Listen Children," by Lucille Clifton, reprinted by permission of Curtis Brown Ltd.; "Incident," by Countee Cullen, reprinted by permission of HarperCollins; "John, Who Is Poor," by Gwendolyn Brooks, reprinted by permission of the author; "Your World," by Georgia Douglas Johnson, reprinted by permission of the author; "Women," "We Alone," and "How Poems Are Made/A Discredited View," by Alice Walker, reprinted by permission of Harcourt Brace; "Those Winter Sundays," by Robert Hayden, reprinted by permission of October House; "Fifth Grade Autobiography" and "Primer," by Rita Dove, reprinted by permission of W. W. Norton; "Little Brown Baby," by Paul Laurence Dunbar, reprinted by permission of HarperCollins; "Rhapsody," by William Stanley Braithwaite, reprinted by permission of the author; "Aunt Sue's Stories" and "My People," by Langston Hughes, reprinted by permission of Harold Ober Associates; "Night" and "Growing Up," by E. Ethelbert Miller, reprinted by permission of Black Classics Press; "Legacies," by Nikki Giovanni, reprinted by permission of William Morrow and Company; "Human Family," by Maya Angelou, reprinted by permission of Random House, Inc.

Permission to reproduce artwork in this book is gratefully acknowledged: p. 7: courtesy of the artist and Francine Seders Gallery; p. 8: courtesy of Lev T. Mills; p.11: collection of DuSable Museum of African American History, Inc.; pp. 12-13, 15, 16-17, 19, 26-27, 32-33, 34-35, 38, 44-45: National Museum of American Art, Washington, DC/Art Resource, NY; pp. 20-21: Hughie Lee-Smith. *Reflection*, 1957, 24 x 36. Oil on particle board. In the collection of the Corcoran Gallery of Art, Washington, DC. The Evans-Tibb Collection, gift of Thurlow Evans Tibbs, Jr., and © Hughie Lee-Smith/licensed by VAGA, New York, NY; p. 22: © Romare Bearden Foundation/licensed by VAGA, New York, NY, and National Museum of American Art, Washington, DC/Art Resource, NY; p.25: Hampton University Museum, Hampton, Virginia; p. 28: © Elizabeth Catlett/licensed by VAGA, New York, NY; pp. 30-31: courtesy of the artist and Francine Seders Gallery; pp. 36-37: Horace Pippin, *Interior*. Gift of Mr. And Mrs. Meyer P. Potamkin, in honor of the fiftieth anniversary of the National Gallery of Art, © 1999 Board of Trustees, National Gallery of Art, Washington, DC, 1944; pp. 40-41: collection of Brandywine River Museum, Betsy James Wyeth Fund; pp. 42-43: Aaron Douglas, *Into Bondage*, 1936, 60 3/8 x 60 1/2. Oil on canvas. In the collection of the Corcoran Gallery of Art, Washington, DC. Museum purchase and partial gift from Thurlow Evans Tibbs, Jr. The Evans-Tibbs Collection, 1996.9.

**Words with Wings**
Compilation copyright © 2001 by Belinda Rochelle
All rights reserved.
Printed in Singapore.
www.harperchildrens.com
Library of Congress Cataloging-in-Publication Data
Words with wings : a treasury of African-American poetry and art / selected by Belinda Rochelle.
p.    cm.
Summary: Pairs twenty works of art by African-American artists with twenty poems by African-American poets.
ISBN 0-688-16415-3 (trade) — ISBN 0-06-029363-2 (library)
1. Children's poetry, American—Afro-American authors.   2. Afro-Americans in art—Juvenile literature.
3. Afro-Americans—Juvenile poetry.   [1. American poetry—Collections.   2. Afro-Americans in art.
3. Afro-Americans—Poetry.]   I. Rochelle, Belinda.
PS591.N4 W67   2001    00-26864
811.008'09282'08996073—dc21   CIP
AC
Designed by Stephanie Bart-Horvath
2   3   4   5   6   7   8   9   10
❖
First Edition

# Contents

# Introduction

The poets and artists represented in *Words with Wings* explore a range of African-American experiences, and, as Maya Angelou reminds us, of experiences shared by all peoples—work, pain, love, anger, regret. They speak of isolation and community, joy and sorrow, the ways people heal or harm one another—but seldom of despair. African-American artists know they cannot afford to give up. As Lucille Clifton says, "1 survive/ survive/ survive."

These artists lived in different places and at different times, but even those who knew one another did not always agree about what it means to be an African-American artist. Should they be content to reveal and record the lives of their people, or should they try to change people's lives? Although Countee Cullen wrote about African-American culture, he wrote in the style of white English and American poets. He believed that was the only proper way to write. Langston Hughes, who wrote at the same time and knew that same poetic tradition, wrote poems influenced by African-American music, especially jazz, and by the rhythms of spoken language. He wanted his poems to reflect the language people spoke on the street, not just the language of poetry books. Gwendolyn Brooks looks at poetry as a vehicle for change: she has held workshops in which gang members wrote poetry.

In "Legacies," a loving grandmother and granddaughter remain unable to say what is in their hearts: ". . . neither of them ever/ said what they meant/ and I guess nobody ever does." But artists—poets, painters, performers—do say what they mean. Sometimes they even say what *we* mean, but are unable or afraid to say. Painters and sculptors allow us to look directly into the eyes of a stranger, or they let us look at the world through their own eyes. Paintings like *The Banjo Lesson* and *Thankful Poor* let us look at private moments without interrupting them.

If, as Georgia Douglas Johnson says, "Your world is as big as you make it," then the poems and paintings in this book enable us to make our worlds bigger. Poems are words with wings, wings made out of words. But we must help give the poems and art their wings by bringing to them our own experiences and histories, and our willingness to let them take us somewhere new.

# auction street

## Lucille Clifton • for angela mcdonald

consider the drum.
consider auction street
and the beat
throbbing up through our shoes,
through the trolley
so that it rides as if propelled
by hundreds, by thousands
of fathers and mothers
led in a coffle
to the block.

consider the block,
topside smooth as skin
almost translucent like a drum
that has been beaten
for the last time
and waits now to be honored
for the music it has had to bear.
then consider brother moses,
who heard from the mountaintop:
take off your shoes,
the ground you walk is holy.

Jacob Lawrence

Gemini I

Lev T. Mills

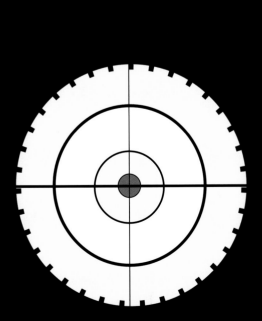

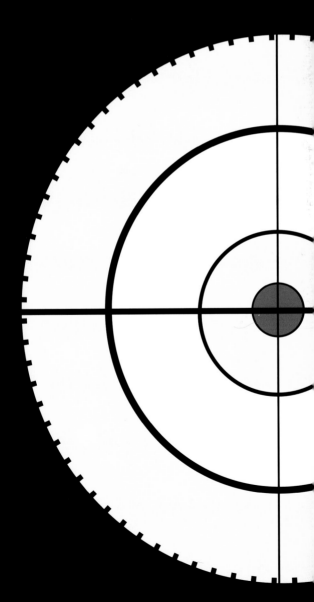

# Incident

## Countee Cullen • for Eric Walrond

Once riding in old Baltimore,
    Heart-filled, head-filled with glee,
I saw a Baltimorean
    Keep looking straight at me.

Now I was eight and very small,
    And he was no whit bigger,
And so I smiled, but he poked out
    His tongue, and called me, "Nigger."

I saw the whole of Baltimore
    From May until December;
Of all the things that happened there
    That's all that I remember.

# John, Who Is Poor

Gwendolyn Brooks

Oh, little children, be good to John!—
Who lives so lone and alone.
Whose Mama must hurry to toil all day.
Whose Papa is dead and done.

Give him a berry, boys, when you may,
And, girls, some mint when you can.
And do not ask when his hunger will end,
Nor yet when it began.

Charles Dawson

Marbles

Landscape with Rainbow

**Robert Scott Duncanson**

# Your World

## Georgia Douglas Johnson

Your world is as big as you make it.
I know, for I used to abide
In the narrowest nest in a corner,
My wings pressing close to my side.

But I sighted the distant horizon
Where the sky line encircled the sea
And I throbbed with a burning desire
To travel this immensity.

I battered the cordons around me
And cradled my wings on the breeze
Then soared to the uttermost reaches
With rapture, with power, with ease!

# Women

Alice Walker

They were women then
My mama's generation
Husky of voice—Stout of
Step
With fists as well as
Hands
How they battered down
Doors
And ironed
Starched white
Shirts
How they led
Armies
Headragged Generals
Across mined
Fields
Booby-trapped
Ditches
To discover books
Desks
A place for us
How they knew what we
*Must* know
Without knowing a page
Of it
Themselves.

**Harriet Tubman**

**William H. Johnson**

Thankful Poor

**Henry Ossawa Tanner**

# Those Winter Sundays

## Robert Hayden

Sundays too my father got up early
and put his clothes on in the blueblack cold,
then with cracked hands that ached
from labor in the weekday weather made
banked fires blaze. No one ever thanked him.

I'd wake and hear the cold splintering, breaking.
When the rooms were warm, he'd call,
and slowly I would rise and dress,
fearing the chronic angers of that house,

Speaking indifferently to him,
who had driven out the cold
and polished my good shoes as well.
What did I know, what I did know
of love's austere and lonely offices?

# listen children

## Lucille Clifton

listen children
keep this in the place
you have for keeping
always
keep it all ways

we have never hated black

listen
we have been ashamed
hopeless      tired      mad
but always
        all ways
we loved us

we have always loved each other
children      all      ways

pass it on

Underground Railroad

William H. Johnson

# Fifth Grade

## Rita Dove

I was four in this photograph fishing
with my grandparents at a lake in Michigan.
My brother squats in poison ivy.
His Davy Crockett cap
sits squared on his head so the raccoon tail
flounces down the back of his sailor suit.

My grandfather sits to the far right
in a folding chair.
and I know his left hand is on
the tobacco in his pants pocket
because I used to wrap it for him
every Christmas. Grandmother's hips
bulge from the brush. she's leaning
into the ice chest, sun through the trees
printing her dress with soft
luminous paws.

I am staring jealously at my brother;
the day before he rode his first horse, alone.
I was strapped in a basket
behind my grandfather.
He smelled of lemons. He's died—

but I remember his hands.

# Autobiography

Lee-Smith
'57

Hughie Lee-Smith

Family

Romare Bearden

# Little Brown Baby

## Paul Laurence Dunbar

Little brown baby wif spa'klin' eyes,
Come to yo' pappy an' set on his knee.
What you been doin', suh—makin' san' pies?
Look at dat bib—You's ez du'ty ez me.
Look at dat mouf—dat's merlasses, I bet;
Come hyeah, Maria, an' wipe off his han's.
Bees gwine to ketch you an' eat you up yit,
Bein' so sticky an' sweet—goodness lan's!

Little brown baby wif spa'klin' eyes,
Who's pappy's darlin' an' who's pappy's chile?
Who is it all de day nevah once tries
Fu' to be cross, er once loses dat smile?
Whah did you git dem teef? My, you's a scamp!
Whah did dat dimple come f'om in yo' chin?
Pappy do' know you—I b'lieves you's a tramp;
Mammy, dis hyeah's some ol' straggler got in!

Let's th'ow him outen de do' in de san',
We do' want stragglers a-layin' 'roun' hyeah;
Let's gin him 'way to de big buggah-man;
I know he's hidin' erroun' hyeah right neah.
Buggah-man, buggah-man, come in de do',
Hyeah's a bad boy you kin have fu' to eat.
Mammy an' pappy do' want him no mo',
Swaller him down f'om his haid to his feet!

Dah, now, I t'ought dat you'd hug me up close.
Go back, ol' buggah, you sha'n't have dis boy.
He ain't no tramp, ner no straggler, of co'se;
He's pappy's pa'dner an' playmate an' joy.
Come to you' pallet now—go to you' res';
Wisht you could allus know ease an' cleah skies;
Wisht you could stay jes' a chile on my breas'—
Little brown baby wif spa'klin' eyes!

# We Alone

Alice Walker

We alone can devalue gold
by not caring
if it falls or rises
in the marketplace.
Wherever there is gold
there is a chain, you know,
and if your chain
is gold
so much the worse
for you.

Feathers, shells
and sea-shaped stones
are all as rare.

This could be our revolution:
to love what is plentiful
as much as
what's scarce.

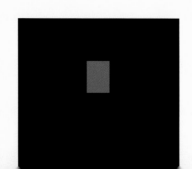

**The Banjo Lesson**

**Henry Ossawa Tanner**

# Rhapsody

## William Stanley Braithwaite

I am glad daylong for the gift of song,
For time and change and sorrow;
For the sunset wings and the world-end things
Which hang on the edge of tomorrow.
I am glad for my heart whose gates apart
Are the entrance-place of wonders,
Where dreams come in from the rush and din
Like sheep from the rains and thunders.

Sharecropper

Elizabeth Catlett

# Aunt Sue's Stories

## Langston Hughes

Aunt Sue has a head full of stories.
Aunt Sue has a whole heart full of
　stories.
Summer nights on the front porch
Aunt Sue cuddles a brown-faced
　child to her bosom
And tells him stories.

Black slaves
Working in the hot sun,
And black slaves
Walking in the dewy night,
And black slaves
Singing sorrow songs on the banks
　of a mighty river
Mingle themselves softly
In the flow of old Aunt Sue's voice,

Mingle themselves softly
In the dark shadows that cross and
　recross
Aunt Sue's stories.

And the dark-faced child, listening,
Knows that Aunt Sue's stories
　are real stories.
He knows that Aunt Sue never got
　her stories
Out of any book at all,
But that they came
Right out of her own life.

The dark-faced child is quiet
Of a summer night
Listening to Aunt Sue's stories.

The Library

Jacob Lawrence

# Primer

Rita Dove

In the sixth grade I was chased home by
the Gatlin kids, three skinny sisters
in rolled-down bobby socks. Hissing
*Brainiac!* and *Mrs. Stringbean!*,
    they trod my heel.
I knew my body was no big deal
but never thought to retort: who's
calling *who* skinny? (Besides, I knew
they'd beat me up.) I survived
their shoves across the schoolyard
because my five-foot-zero mother drove up
in her Caddie to shake them down to size.
Nothing could get me into that car.
I took the long way home, swore
I'd show them all: I would grow up.

# How Poems Are Made

## A Discredited View

### Alice Walker

Letting go
in order to hold on
I gradually understand
how poems are made.

There is a place the fear must go.
There is a place the choice must go.
There is a place the loss must go.
The leftover love.
The love that spills out
of the too full cup
and runs and hides
its too full self
in shame.

I gradually comprehend
how poems are made.
To the upbeat flight of memories.
The flagged beats of the running
heart.

I understand how poems are made.
They are the tears
that season the smile.
The stiff-neck laughter
that crowds the throat.
The leftover love.

I know how poems are made.
There is a place the loss must go
There is a place the gain must go.
The leftover love.

School's Out

**Allan Rohan Crite**

# this morning
## (for the girls of eastern high school)

Lucille Clifton

this morning
this morning
        i met myself
coming in

a bright
jungle girl
shining
quick as a snake
a tall
tree girl a
me girl
        i met myself
this morning
coming in

and all day
i have been
a black bell
ringing
i survive
        survive
survive

# Night

### E. Ethelbert Miller

at some ungodly hour
her house shoes would scrape across
the wooden floor
as she moved from bedroom to kitchen
i would lie in my room and hear her
opening cabinets
washing dishes
placing a pot on the stove
then walking slowly back to where I was
to see how i was sleeping
to see if any blankets were on the floor

H. PiPPiN,

GAMIN

Augusta Savage

# Growing Up

E. Ethelbert Miller

the day my mother
threw away my comic books
and encouraged me to read the bible
was the day i gave up being
a superhero and started to think
of miracles

this is how i came to love you
like moses looking over his
shoulder before he left that
mountain

Horace Pippin

# Legacies

## Nikki Giovanni

her grandmother called her from the playground
   "yes, ma'am"
   "i want chu to learn how to make rolls" said the old
woman proudly
but the little girl didn't want
to learn how because she knew
even if she couldn't say it that
that would mean when the old one died she would be less
dependent on her spirit so
she said
   "i don't want to know how to make no rolls"
with her lips poked out
and the old woman wiped her hands on
her apron saying "lord
   these children"
and neither of them ever
said what they meant
and i guess nobody ever does

[27 jan 72]

**Aaron Douglas**

Langston Hughes

# My

The night is beautiful,
So the faces of my people.

The stars are beautiful,
So the eyes of my people.

Beautiful, also, is the sun.
Beautiful, also, are the souls of my people.

# People

# Human Family

## Maya Angelou

I note the obvious differences
in the human family.
Some of us are serious,
some thrive on comedy.

Some declare their lives are lived
as true profundity,
and others claim they really live
the real reality.

The variety of our skin tones
can confuse, bemuse, delight,
brown and pink and beige
   and purple,
tan and blue and white.

I've sailed upon the seven seas
and stopped in every land,
I've seen the wonders of the world,
not yet one common man.

I know ten thousand women
called Jane and Mary Jane,
but I've not seen any two
who really were the same.

Mirror twins are different
although their features jibe,
and lovers think quite different
   thoughts
while lying side by side.

We love and lose in China,
we weep on England's moors,
and laugh and moan in Guinea,
and thrive on Spanish shores.

We seek success in Finland,
are born and die in Maine.
In minor ways we differ,
in major we're the same.

I note the obvious differences
between each sort and type,
but we are more alike, my friends,
than we are unalike.

We are more alike, my friends,
than we are unalike.

We are more alike, my friends,
than we are unalike.

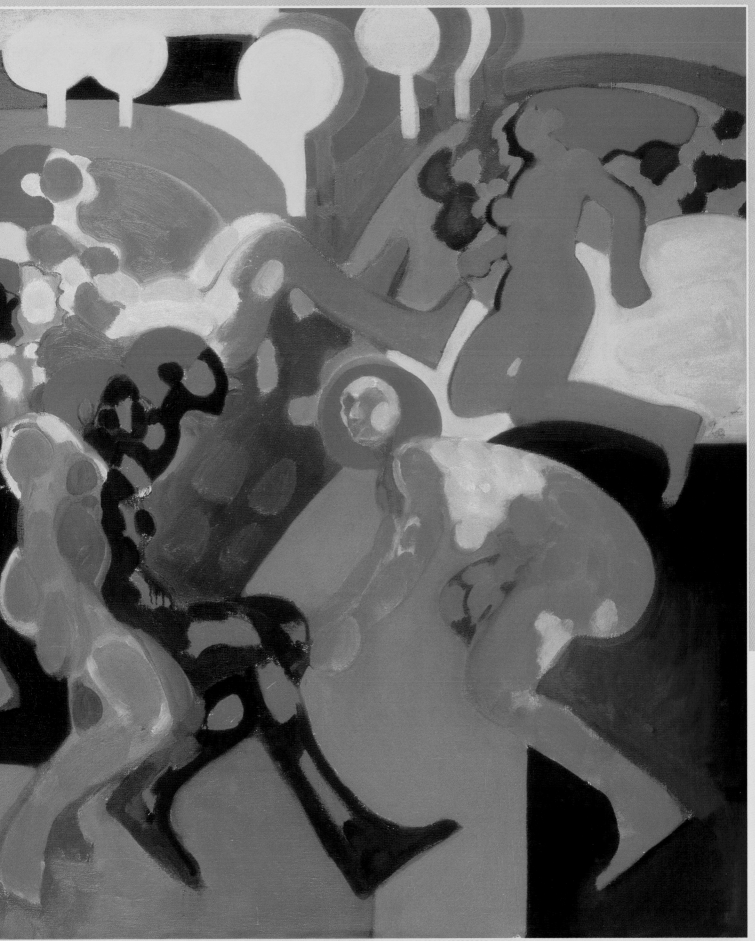

**Figurative Composition #7**

**Emilio Cruz**

# About the Poets and Artists

**Maya Angelou** (1928- ) says, "The main thing in one's own private world is to try to laugh as much as you cry." This must sometimes have been difficult for her. For five years of her childhood in rural Arkansas she became unable to speak at all. Since then she has spoken and written a great deal, often about strength, courage, pride, and overcoming obstacles. Angelou has worked as a waitress, a dancer, an actress, and San Francisco's first African-American streetcar conductor. She has written a five-volume autobiography, many books of poetry, and productions for stage, television, and film. At the request of Bill Clinton, she wrote the poem "On the Pulse of Morning," which she read at his 1993 presidential inauguration.

Born in Charlotte, North Carolina, **Romare Bearden** (1913-1988) created paintings and collages that celebrate the daily life, ceremonies, and rituals of the many black communities he knew from childhood summers in rural North Carolina; his grandmother's boardinghouse in Pittsburgh, near the steel mills; and Harlem, where he lived from his early adolescence through the flowering of the Harlem Renaissance, a movement of black art, literature, and music of the 1920s. Bearden's influences included the whole history of western painting, American quilts, Chinese painting, African sculpture, and blues and jazz. "Art celebrates a victory," Bearden once said—though the victory could be that of overcoming pain.

**William Stanley Braithwaite** (1878-1962) was born in Boston, Massachusetts, to West Indian parents. He was a poet, an anthologist, a novelist, and a biographer. He was also a professor at Atlanta University. Like Countee Cullen and Robert Hayden, he wanted to be considered a poet, not a black poet, but he served as a mentor to other African Americans who were writers, including Langston Hughes and Paul Laurence Dunbar.

**Gwendolyn Brooks** (1917- ) was born in Topeka, Kansas, but her family moved to Chicago when she was young, and she lives there still. She began writing poetry when she was seven and published her first poem at thirteen. In 1950 Brooks became the first African American to win the Pulitzer Prize for poetry. Although she often wrote about black characters, she says that her understanding of what it means to be a black poet changed when she met politically active black writers at a 1967 writers' conference. After that Brooks began holding writing workshops for inner-city gang members, and many of her poems since then reflect her desire that her poetry both reveal and change people's lives.

**Elizabeth Catlett** (1919- ) was born in Washington, D.C. She received her B.A. from Howard University and her master of fine arts—the first one ever awarded—from the University of Iowa. W. E. B. DuBois told her, "Never take a step backward or you'll never stop running." Catlett was always most interested in creating sculptures, paintings, and prints of black women: mothers and children, women from black history, individuals like the black child in her famous lithograph *Negro es Bello (Black Is Beautiful)*. "My art is to serve black people," she says. "That's one of my main aims."

**Lucille Clifton** (1936- ) was born in Depew, New York. Her mother wrote poetry, and her father told the stories of their family's history, which he could trace back to West Africa. Clifton was thirty-three years old and had six children under the age of ten when she published her first book. Since then she has published many, for children and for adults, including a series of picture books about a boy named Everett Anderson.

**Allan Rohan Crite** (1918- ) was born in New Jersey but studied art in Boston, made his career there, and lives there still. He is best known for his paintings of the everyday lives of African Americans in Boston in the 1920s and 1930s. His neighbors called him the "reporter-artist" because his paintings showed the details of their lives—clothing, expressions, buildings—with great accuracy. During the 1940s, Crite began to depict religious themes in his work. His paintings are represented in several major museum collections.

**Emilio Cruz** (1938- ) was born in the Bronx, New York. A painter and a performance artist, he has been influenced by a tremendously wide range of subjects, including western and eastern philosophy, art history, and mythology. His paintings are expressionistic. In expressionism, artists depict their emotions rather than showing how things look realistically. Cruz tends to emphasize similarities rather than differences among people, and he believes that art must speak to the human spirit, to something that all people have in common.

**Countee Cullen** (1903?-1946) was raised in New York City. After completing a master of arts at Harvard University and a fellowship in Paris, he returned to New York. He identified himself as a *poet*, not a black poet, and wrote in the tradition of (mostly white) British and American poetry. He believed strongly that poets who wrote in dialect separated themselves from the "heritage of the English language." Cullen was, however, equally strong in his support for other African Americans who were poets, and he edited an early, important collection of their work. He also wrote often and powerfully against racism.

Born in Brunswick, Georgia, **Charles Dawson** (1889-1940) was a painter, illustrator, sculptor, and a staff artist on a newspaper. He studied art in New York

City and in Chicago. Throughout much of his career, Dawson painted portraits of African Americans—historical figures as well as contemporary people who paid him to paint their picture. He published the *A.B.C. of Great Negroes*, illustrated with linoleum block prints, when few such books existed. During the Depression, when federal funds were available for artists, Dawson did many illustrations of children.

**Beauford Delaney** (1901?-1979) was born in Knoxville, Tennessee. Delaney painted in a number of artistic styles—more than most African-American artists. Some of his works are portraits, others are abstracts, but throughout his career he consistently used bright colors in his paintings. He lived in New York in the 1940s, where he painted his Greenwich Village friends and also homeless people. In the 1950s he moved to Paris, where he served as a mentor to many black artists who came from the United States to study in Europe. By this time his paintings were abstract. Abstraction, he explained, could be a way of getting to the real truth of a thing, revealing it more clearly than a picture of its form could.

**Aaron Douglas** (1899-1979) was born and raised in Topeka, Kansas. He studied art in Nebraska, New York, and Paris. Douglas is recognized as one of the leading artists of the Harlem Renaissance. When he arrived in New York City in 1925, civil rights leaders W. E. B. DuBois and Charles S. Johnson commissioned him to illustrate editorials in their magazines. In his magazine and book illustrations, book covers, and murals showing the history of African Americans, Douglas created an African-influenced art that was unlike the work of any other artist of his time.

**Rita Dove** (1952-) was born in Akron, Ohio, and began writing plays and stories while in junior high school. *Thomas and Beulah*, a book of narrative poems inspired by events in the lives of her grandparents, won the Pulitzer Prize for poetry in 1986. As well as poems, Dove has published plays, a novel, and a collection of short stories. Some of her writings are autobiographical; others, like *Thomas and Beulah*, show the richness and complexity of the inner lives of poor people. Dove, a professor at the University of Virginia, has received numerous awards and honors. When President Clinton appointed her poet laureate of the United States in 1993, she was the first woman and the first African American to be given that honor; she was also the first person ever to be appointed for two terms.

**Paul Laurence Dunbar** (1872-1906) was born in Dayton, Ohio, the son of former slaves who told him stories of their lives and experiences. Dunbar used this knowledge of his heritage in his poems, stories, and novels. Despite his success as a student and his talent as a writer, Dunbar worked for a time as an elevator operator and had to borrow money to publish his first book of poems, which he sold in the elevator for a dollar. His 1896 collection, *Lyrics of the Lowly Life*, made him internationally famous. Dunbar wrote some of his poems in the spoken language of African Americans, which angered some readers but inspired others.

**Robert Scott Duncanson** (1817?-1872) was born in Cincinnati, Ohio, and became a painter when many African Americans were still enslaved. As a young man he worked in his family's house-painting and decorating business. In the 1840s he began to be hired to paint portraits; he also painted landscapes and scenes from history. Eventually he studied art in Italy and Scotland and gained a reputation in Canada and Europe. His best-known works are landscapes, some of them based on famous literary works of his time.

**Nikki Giovanni** (1943-) was born in Knoxville, Tennessee, and raised in Cincinnati, Ohio. She began to work for the civil rights movement while she was a student at Fisk University and has remained committed to social justice for African Americans and for women. Her early poetry reflected the anger and political beliefs of the black rights movement and was specifically about social action. Her later poems are as likely to be about family and love as about politics, but she believes that these poems are as radical as her earlier ones.

**Robert Hayden** (1913-1980), like Countee Cullen, wished to be read and judged not as a black poet but as a poet who was, among other things, black. Although themselves uneducated, his parents supported his desire to write. Perhaps it is not surprising that, having struggled so hard to get an education, he wanted to write in the language and style of an educated man. Hayden read widely in British and American poetry, including the poetry of the Harlem Renaissance, and he liked to tell stories in his poems.

**Langston Hughes** (1902-1967), a key figure in the Harlem Renaissance, was born in Joplin, Missouri. He lived and worked in many states and countries before settling in New York City. Hughes wrote at the same time as Countee Cullen, but unlike Cullen he wanted to create a new literature that expressed the African-American language and culture, and he wove into his poems the sounds of black voices and music. Hughes also wrote novels, operettas, history books, newspaper columns, children's books, autobiographies, and short stories. Although his critics feared that his writings about poor blacks would reinforce racial stereotypes, Hughes's life and work challenged these stereotypes and inspired other writers. "Words should be used to make people *believe* and *do*," wrote Hughes.

Although she is recognized as a poet of the Harlem Renaissance, **Georgia Douglas Johnson** (1886-1966) never lived in New York City. Born in Rome, Georgia, she lived much of her life in Washington, D.C., moving there when her husband accepted a government appointment from President Taft. After her husband's death she remained for many years in Washington, working at various jobs, writing poetry, short stories, and a newspaper column, and maintaining a Saturday evening literary salon where African-American writers such as Langston Hughes could talk and read their poems.

**William H. Johnson** (1901-1970) was born in Florence, South Carolina. He studied art with some of the great painters of his time; however, like some other artists of the period he was interested in and influenced by primitive art. In his best-known paintings, of African Americans on farms and in the city and of historical figures, the people and objects appear flat, not three-dimensional. Johnson lived for many years in Denmark and Sweden, and his paintings were admired internationally. Johnson became mentally ill in 1947 and he was confined to a mental institution from then until his death, but the work he left behind is an important contribution to art history.

**Jacob Lawrence** (1917-2000) was born in New Jersey, but his family moved to New York City when he was twelve. As he was developing as an artist, Lawrence was surrounded by the rich culture of the Harlem Renaissance. His knowledge of African and African-American literature and art influenced his choice of subjects. Lawrence is known for his large series of paintings based on the lives of famous black people, on African-American history, and on life in Harlem. Lawrence was the first African-American artist to be exhibited in major New York galleries and is probably the best-known African-American artist of the twentieth century.

**Hughie Lee-Smith** (1915-) was born in Eustis, Florida. His family recognized his talent when he was young and supported his development as an artist, for which he remains grateful. Trained in classical art, he received fellowships and grants that allowed him to support himself, yet his work did not become widely known until he had been painting for fifty years. His paintings almost always show people—usually black, sometimes white—alone and isolated. Even when he portrays city streets, the scenes echo with loneliness. He says, "In my case, aloneness, I think, has stemmed from the fact that I'm black."

**E. Ethelbert Miller** (1950-) was born in Washington, D.C. In his eight books of poetry, he writes about a wide range of subjects: his family, love, baseball, social justice, the assassination of Malcolm X. As the director of the African American Studies Resource Center at Howard University, he has immersed himself in African-American culture. "In some ways I modeled myself after Langston Hughes," Miller has said. "He was the writer who best embodied and articulated the hope and dreams of our people." Like Hughes, Miller draws on oral and written literary traditions and has been influenced by music, from blues and jazz to the songs of protest singers like Phil Ochs and Bob Dylan.

**Lev T. Mills** (1940-) was born in a small town in Florida. He studied art in Florida, Wisconsin, London, Paris, and New York. Mills says he has always been more interested in creating art that moves people deeply than in creating political statements. He wants viewers to have to think about what his art means. Mills has been an art teacher; he has also been hired to create sculptures and tile murals for public places around Atlanta, where he now lives.

**Horace Pippin** (1888-1946) was born in West Chester, Pennsylvania. As a boy he enjoyed drawing, but his family could not afford to train him as an artist. After fighting in World War I in a famous all-black infantry division, Pippin returned to the United States with a shattered right arm and no civil rights. In emotional and physical pain, he discovered that he could draw on a wood panel using a hot poker. He then began painting, holding the brush in his right hand and pushing it with his left arm. His earliest paintings show the ugliness of war. His later paintings include landscapes; portraits; and family scenes, some of them based on childhood memories; scenes from African-American history; and, during World War II, antiwar pictures. His work earned him the respect of other artists, both for his artistic techniques and for his portrayal of African-American life.

**Augusta Savage** (1900-1962) was born in Green Cove, Florida, the seventh of fourteen children. Her father, a poor Methodist minister, would have preferred her to pursue something more practical than sculpture, but all her life Savage fought for her art and often fought to help other artists too. In high school she taught her fellow students how to work with clay; she then moved to New York City to study art. After years of supporting herself by working in factories and laundries, she won a scholarship that allowed her to study in Paris. Returning to New York, she founded the Savage School of Arts and Crafts in Harlem. Much of Savage's work has been lost and now exists only in photographs.

**Charles Searles** (1937-) was born in Philadelphia, Pennsylvania. A painter who later became a sculptor, Searles says that he was first influenced by African sculpture and by the paintings of Jacob Lawrence. While studying at the Pennsylvania Academy of Fine Arts, he won an award that allowed him to visit Ghana, Morocco, and Nigeria. There he discovered that "art was in the people," and his work after this time was influenced by African fabrics, music, dance, and masks. As he has developed as an artist, Searles has been inspired by images and ideas from many other cultures. He has also been influenced by the music he listens to while he creates his art and by his own work as a musician.

**Henry Ossawa Tanner** (1859-1937) was born into a middle-class family in Pittsburgh, Pennsylvania. The son of a bishop, he was expected to become a minister. Many of his works reflect his religious upbringing and Christian ideals. As well as painting biblical scenes, he painted pictures of ordinary people—including those in *Thankful Poor* and *The Banjo Lesson*—in a manner that offered a different way of looking at people who until recently had been enslaved. The people in his paintings are poor, but they are free and they have dignity.

**Alice Walker** (1944-) was born in Eatonton, Georgia, to poor parents. She won the Pulitzer Prize for fiction and the American Book Award for her novel *The Color Purple*, but not until her parents had seen the film did they read the novel. "My family is not a reading family," says Walker. Raised in the segregated South, Walker became a novelist, a poet, a mother, and a civil rights activist during the 1960s. She has also published short stories and a collection of essays. Writing of older black women writers and activists, Walker says, "They are like jewels. We are richer because we have these women."